Net Loss

a Florida commercial fisherman's saga

text by

Evelyn Wilde Mayerson

illustrations by

Philip S. Steel

LONG WIND PUBLISHING, LLC
FT. PIERCE, FL

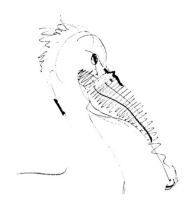

First Printing, 2004

Designed and Edited by Jon Ward

Net Loss; A Florida commercial fisherman's saga
Evelyn Wilde Mayerson,
Philip S. Steel,
ISBN 1-892695-15-4

Long Wind Publishing, LLC
108 North Depot Drive
Ft. Pierce, FL 34950
(772) 595-0268
www.LongWindPub.com

Printed in Hong Kong

Cover and Title Page painting:"Casting the Net", 24"w x 36" H, oil on canvas

With grateful thanks to Grier MacFarland for her research assistance, to Dr. Grant Gilmore, Dr. Mary Rice, Lieutenant Steve Arcuri, Mike Jepson and George Geiger for their expertise, to commercial and sports fishermen Glen Black, Glenda Black Macon, Rubert Harden, Ray Allen Harden, Mike Gruber, Chris Hegedus, Terry Parsons, Johnny Jones, Sam Hegedus and Robert (Moby) Paul for their experience, to reporter Sheila Lowenstein, for sharing her notes, to Kathleen Slesnick for providing access to the historical archives of Ft. Pierce and St. Lucie County and to Don Mayerson for thinking up the title. Personal appreciation to Joan Steel and to Leo Henriquez for believing in this project.

"Fisherman's Home", 24"h x 36"w, oil on canvas.

Much wiser folk than me have long observed that one of life's few constants is change and nowhere on this whirling blue orb is that more true than in Florida. Many people only flirt with her, as tourists, passing through quickly, glancing at her, but not really seeing her. They see a place of fun, of distraction. However, for some families, she is the multi-generational source of traditional livlihoods that are constantly being pressured to change faster than I can get these words down on paper. Fishing, like ranching, has long been a lifestyle in this state, with fathers and grandfathers teaching sons and grandsons, and even granddaughters, to be watermen. In the 1990's, a host of different concerns combined to force a fundamental sociological change on this traditional way of life. A ban on certain kinds of net fishing demanded that whole families reexamine how they would spend the productive working days of the rest of their lives. Methods of fishing that had been practiced for five, six, even seven generations were no longer an option.

Philip Steel and Evelyn Wilde Mayerson, artists from two completely different disciplines, chose to focus on this story through the prism of their art. Traveling on fishing boats, visiting the fish houses and listening to the comments of fishing families inspired Steel, a renowned painter, to create this collection of evocative images portraying people hard at work at a living that's also a love. On seeing the graphic representation of a lifestyle in transition, Mayerson drew on her considerable talents as a novelist and playwright to fashion a one-man play that made the paintings come alive and gave voice to the mute witnesses. The play toured Florida, and for a brief shining moment, longsuffering fishermen found a champion in art, for the show inspired passionate comment on their prospects for survival and held up an inspired mirror on the dignity of a life's work.

Jon Ward, Director of Cultural Affairs
St. Lucie County, Florida

"White Boots and Bucket", 18"h x 24"w, oil on board.

Net Loss

A Play in Monologue Form

I've been fishing these waters for thirty-five years. Forty, if you count the times I played hookey from school with a pelican riding on my engine and a curtain of rain drifting east from Lake Okeechobee...me, keeping a sharp lookout for a flashing mass of silver taking double somersaults in the air. That's when I learned how to draw the State of Florida. An upside down turkey with Lake Okeechobee for its eye.

Ft. Pierce was once a military fort, built of palmetto logs and pitch on the site of an old Indian mound, part of a whole network of forts, crisscrossing the State of Florida, one day's march apart. The U.S.Army was fighting the Seminoles back then. Chasing them Indians from one end of the State to the other. Most everything is chased by something. Frogs chase bugs. Fish chase frogs. Gators chase fish or little dogs. Gators love little dogs, particularly those with their leashes still attached. Gator, he winds up as a pair of shoes or a lady's purse.

My great-great-granddaddy was sent here from Charleston to fight the Third Seminole War. I was named after him. Wade Curtis. My momma gave me the middle name of Ray because, she said, I brought sunshine into her life. My great-great-grandaddy liked the Indian River so much he settled on the edge of Moore's Creek. Leastways, where Moore's Creek used to be, winding and curving its way west, before a couple of engineers thought they better straighten it out and put an end to it's meandering.

The river was full of fish, scales glistening like silver in water as clear as gin. Scrub cattle rooting wild in the palmetto. Ducks so plentiful they sat on the water like rafts. Mosquitoes so thick they hung on your eyelashes. Which is why St. Lucie County was named Mosquito County. That's before official folks realized that they better give the county another name if they wanted settlers.

My great-great-grandaddy received a commendation from General Robert E. Lee, himself. For dousing the lantern in the Jupiter lighthouse, so the Confederate blockade runners could outwit the Yankees. No one can pin down for sure the part about Robert E. Lee, but leastways, that's what they tell me.

My great-grandaddy used to go plume hunting until Audubon folks started agitating and the State of Florida passed a law against it. That just drove the prices up. From where I sit, law was passed to quiet down the Yankees.

A few other Yankee ideas took hold. Take the old Ft. Pierce Coast Guard Station. Build according to the way they built things up north. Which meant "no" to a front porch and "yes" to a basement. I don't have to tell you what happens to a basement in St. Lucie County. It fills up with water. Regularly. Like some kind of indoor grotto coated with those tiny black mud snails, moving as they feed, until someone gets around to pump the water out, along with the snails.

Dusty Boy", 24"h x 36"w, oil on canvas.

Commercial fishing began in my granddaddy's time, just about the time Audubon folks started all that agitation about them plume birds. Two events gave fishing its kickstart. The first was the frost of 1894 and ninety-five that ruined the citrus and the pineapple. I heard stories of raccoons froze to death with their mouths wide open. Of trails leading north, filled with families in oxcarts, heading back into Georgia and Alabama, looking for work that didn't depend on a drop in temperature that could turn an orange into a ball of ice.

The second event that got fishing off to a flying start was the arrival of the railroad in Titusville. Fish were in the waters for the taking. Turtles weighing more than 150 pounds were caught and butchered just for the meat in their flippers. And Mr. Flagler's iced fish cars delivered the catch to market before it turned. Fish were five cents a pound, going as high as thirty-five cents if the fish were barreled.

Everyone started building fishing boats. Wood for the ribs came from someplace up north but the rest of the boat was homegrown. Cedar for planking came from Tallahassee and the black mangrove for the bowstem came from Hutchinson Island.

Fish houses were built all over the river. Titusville. Eau Gallie. Sebastian. Ft. Pierce. Stuart. There's still a few around, patched with tarpaper, hanging lopsided, like they had one too many. Thirty years ago, there were fifteen fish houses in Ft. Pierce, alone. Now, there are only three.

"Early Morning", 36"h x 48"w, oil on board.

When I was a little kid, pompano would come skipping over the water like river stones. You could get all the big fat mullet you wanted with a spear or a cast net. My daddy added lamp black to the nets to make them darker and harder for the fish to see.

We spoke a charm.

Cast it over the water like the bread they talk about in the Bible.

"Fishy, fishy bite.
Your mother said you could
Your father said you would
Fishy, fishy bite."

If you were real lazy, you could leave a lantern burning in a tethered rowboat and a half dozen mullet would jump in. If you didn't have a lantern, a blazing pitch pine basket would do just fine. Mullet was scared of both.

If you were lazy . . . and a little touched in the head, like my Uncle Billy . . . you threw in a stick of dynamite. Once, Billy carried two sticks, lit one, threw in the wrong stick and wound up floating senseless alongside the fish.

That's when I believed that if you dropped a horse hair in a pail of water, it would turn into a snake. My sister and I would watch over a bucket while that horse hair drifted this way and that. We watched 'til nightfall. I'll tell you this. Waiting for these fishing laws to be repealed is like waiting for that horse hair to turn into a snake. It ain't never gonna happen.

"Katie Marie in Storm", 17.5"h x 48"w, oil on board.

"Fishing for Mackeral", 36"h x 48"w, oil on canvas.

The government says fish stocks are dwindling and that we're to blame. For bringing in too many fish. Seems they ought to look to themselves. For dredging canals that carry dirty runoff into the river. For letting developers rip away the mangrove. Where do they think the fish are gonna spawn? Next to some seawall? Even the fish need privacy.

What I don't understand is why they let foreigners fish out our waters so that we have to import fish from the other side of the world. A lot of foolishness, if you ask me. Fish nobody ever heard of. Borbouni. Lovraki. Dorado. Barramundi. Fast food folks are paying air freight to fly in Hoki. Who wants to eat a fish that sounds like something you spray up your nose?

You take countries like Russia and China. They got billions of people to feed and let's face it, neither one was never what you'd call a team player. They're making fishing an industry. They're sending out great big old fishing fleets to pick our waters clean. There's no place for the fish to hide.

Then, you got doctors heating up the other end of the problem. That's right, doctors. They're the ones who had to go and tell folks that eating fish was healthy. That's what drove up consumption. Between the doctors and the Chinese, it's a squeeze play.

"Smitty", 24"h x 30"w, oil on canvas.

Smitty here, he likes to swap stories. He's talking to a trucker. A fella who bragged that he could drive an L.A. turnaround in two days. If you think Smitty and the trucker don't have much in common, then I got to remind you that even bass and aligator hang together.

Don't ask me why. All I know is, you see a couple of 'gators in a pond, especially if they're up on four legs, you can count on catching you some bass. Told that to a fella from New Jersey. He said one alligator trotting like a dog was all he needed to hightail it out of there, bass or no bass.

Knew he was from somewhere up north without him saying one word. I was hunkered down, sitting back on my heels, lighting my smoke by scratching a thumbnail across the head of a match, cupped in the palm of my hand. He couldn't do neither one. Couldn't get that match to light, couldn't hunker down without rolling backwards on his butt. Has to do with design. Cracker menfolks like me, we got this slat rump, hard as siding. New Jersey fella, well, the meat on him just pulled him down.

This New Jersey fella showed me his watch. Stuck it in my face like it was a squirt clam. Thing works underwater. With all kinds of dials glowing like gulf weed. Hell, fisherman don't need no watch, underwater or on top of it. Fishermen tell time by the tide. If the tide was dead low at three in the afternoon, the next week, it'll be high in the afternoon, and low at night. See, the tide reverses itself every week, something like these regulations I got to abide with.

These permits, for example. You need a State permit to fish. You also need a Federal permit. Federal permit means a specific license for a specific fish. Kingfish, wahoo, tuna, you name it. A snapper/grouper permit costs twelve thousand dollars! You can't even buy a snapper/grouper permit until the year 2005 unless you want to buy one from an individual who doesn't want to fish anymore. But, he's gonna set his own price. Anyhow, a fisherman needs two Federal permits to fish legally. You don't need to be a rocket scientist to know that they're trying to cut our numbers in half.

"Live Shrimp", 24"h x 30"w, oil on canvas.

Tides are better than any clock, give or take fifteen minutes. Only exceptions are gale tides. Folks on shore know a gale is coming if they see a cat on a fence. Another sign is crabs scurrying out of the mangroves. Or birds flying low, ants covering their anthills, a ring around the moon. A hurricane, now that's another story. June, too soon. July, stand by. August, look out you must. September, remember. October, all over.

Best land sign of a hurricane is a good mango crop.

You can see signs of a hurricane for days ahead, at sea. The wind drops. Ocean is flat, except for swirls of current, like a pot trying to boil. There is a great canyon of clouds and the mullet rush out the inlet, into the ocean, where they know it's safe. If they can't make it out, they wind up twitching on the shore, with mud in their gills. Bet you didn't know a mullet has a gizzard. Mullet likes to munch on algae and needs his gizzard to sift out the sand. Mullet munching on algae is no big thing. Fish will take all kinds of bait.

I know a fella lives in an old fishing shack that him and his brother hauled back from the river-bank. Turned it into a bait house. Sells a dozen shrimp for a buck and a quarter. Keeps a sign over his register that says, "If everybody knows your business, you won't have it for very long." Here he's sitting with all that shrimp and he'd druther catch carp with doughballs.

Except he doesn't fish anymore. Too much paperwork. When he's not selling bait, he's working in concrete. It's hot as Hell, pouring all that concrete in the sun, no sea breeze to cool you off. Only thing worse is roofing.

I asked him if he misses the work. Figured he's say no. Fishing is hard. On your feet all day, hear-ing that engine banging away, hauling fish over the side, eighty miles out for four, five days at a time. Once in awhile, a piece of gear breaks, a squall comes up out of nowhere.

He surprised me. Told me what he misses most is bringing in a big fish. When the surface of the ocean bulges, then bursts, like it's giving birth, hundreds of clucking coots roosting on the waves, then taking to the air, running on the surface of the water, flapping their wings and kicking to get up. Him, yanking hard with both hands, gaining a yard of line, yanking again, swinging with all his might, each arm on the cord, left, right, the tail of the fish slapping and banging, thumping its life out against the planking, the whole boat shivering like it had a fever.

Now whenever I see him, he's scuttling back to his house like a ghost crab popping back into it's hole.

Trout fishermen used to muffle their oars with burlap, then go to fish, quiet as all get-out, beating the water in front of their lure with a splasher. The idea was, they confused the trout with a commotion in the water. That's what all these agencies are doing. Making a commotion in the water so no one will know what they're really up to. Which is . . . to put me out of business. Pure and simple.

Today's Florida fishing industry is a sorry mess. Seems like the only way we can catch enough to earn a living is against the law. By the time we get through the red tape and the permits, then we're told we can't fish where the fish are. Fishing is like gambling. You can't see 'em until you catch 'em. You just have to believe that they're there and that they're hungry and maybe stupid enough to confuse a metal lure for a cricket.

It's a Cops and Robbers game where there are more cops than robbers. You have to work with quotas from the Department of Natural Resources. You have to log every entry, like a bookkeeper. There are catch limits for certain kinds of fish. Regulations from the State and Federal Fish and Wildlife Departments, the Department of Weights and Measures, conservation folks and all the ruckus created by the sports fishemen. Add that to the fact that fish populations are not as good as they once were, and it makes it harder and harder to make a living catching fish.

A fortune teller once read my palm, told me I was going to have a long life. What she was reading were the deep creased scars from handling heavy fish on the cords. She was reading the marlin I used to catch. You ever see a marlin close, jumping high in the air, his sword as long as a baseball bat, his pectoral fins, lavender, the color of an Easter egg? Seeing them is all you can do now. You can't bring 'em to the dock.

Best remedy for a sliced finger is plain old pine oil unless it's begun to throb and then you make a poultice of sugar and turpentine. The fella who told me that was my daddy's best friend. He quit fishing five, ten years back. Last I heard, he was a groundskeeper at Dodgertown. It isn't so bad. Leastways, that's what his wife says. He gets to see all the games. Even got him an autograph or two.

It doesn't matter how many callouses you have, how many welts you have from man-of-war. When you reach out for a line, rub it softly between your thumb and forefinger. You can always feel the pull. And, even when you let the line slip between your fingers, the fish never feels any tension.

That's the reason fishermen know their way around womenfolk. A fisherman always senses the first pull. It's more like a tremble, a shiver . . . and, since he's smart, he waits. He gets a nibble, he reaches out for the line, feels it softly between his thumb and forefinger. He knows not to yank it in . . . he knows to let it slip between his fingers, rolling off reserve coils, dropping a hook over the side and making it fast to a ring bolt in the stern. Maybe he even baits another line and leaves it coiled in the shade of the bow.

He's waiting for the right moment to start working the fish!

Two of these guys used to bring in shark. Hoisted them on block and tackle, soaked the hides in brine, then sent them to China. I hear shark's hide is a delicacy to Chinese folk. Same as baby back ribs is to us. After they cut off the fins and the hide, they took out the shark's liver. You can believe it or not, but a shark's liver is good for fourteen gallons of oil.

This fella here could sound fish clear across the river, particularly on a calm night, with smoke rising and a screech owl hooting from some rooftop. I watched him when I was a kid, watched his circle of net get smaller and smaller. Watched a silver flashing of thrashing, fluttering fish forced into a pocket.

Here, he's bringing in swordfish. Getting ready to put a knee on the carcass and cut, from the back of the head to the tail, from the backbone to the belly. I know for sure those other two would rather be hauling in shark.

I like it when my boat is rocking gently at anchor. Light breeze from the southeast. In the water below, strap-bladed turtle grass swaying in the current. In the shallows, sea cucumber and spider crabs, all mixed up in a tangle of battered lobster traps and old shrimp netting, studded with seaweed. The water has music of it's own. There's the sound of the river sucking at the mangroves. The chug of sewage being pumped from the city's drainpipes.

Sometimes, out on the water, you look up and see pelicans and buzzards, soaring in circles over your head. Showboating in the sky, looking to see how far up they can get that updraft to take them, free of charge. Then you look down, alongside your boat, and see a dolphin with it's shiny gold head, playing in the water . . . water the same kind of blue as the sky. And you think the sky and the water are the same, one up, one down, and sometimes, you can't even tell which is which.

It's like standing on the edge of the universe and looking out at all that is or ever was.

There was a letter to the editor in the newspaper. It said that the regulators don't care nothin' about the environment. That they're keeping the fish for the sports fishermen. I don't know how true that is. I do know that the recreational fishermen were the ones who could lobby, the ones who got the legislator's ears. They catch trout, then release 'em. You know what happens to trout when you unhook 'em in the summer? Well, most of 'em die.

Propaganda put us out of business. We should have fought for ourselves. That's the American way.

The bartender at Casey's showed me a survey, published by the Marine Recreational Fisheries. It's all about yellowtail snapper. They said, right there in black and white, that the recreational fisherman catches ten pounds for every pound that we catch. The sports fisherman's quota is higher than mine. It's not fair. They sell lots of their catch to restaurants.

I don't have anything against charter boats, personally, mind you. Two or three of my friends make their living strapping tourists into fighting chairs. They got to pay the rent, same as me.

I know this young fella, his grandaddy and his daddy and two of his uncles. His mother, Verna, makes apple beer as good as any I've ever had. Dries her peelings in the sun, puts them in a crock and lets it sit. When it's ready, it's as sweet as it can be. Verna swears she doesn't add a drop of sugar.

Verna's boy is as smart as a whip. Knew everything about fishing before he learned to shave. He's got all kinds of equipment on his boat … radar, sonar. But, that's not why he's good. He's good because he learned to follow the birds. The birds go after the bait, wherever the bait is, that's where the big fish are, coming in to feed.

That's the thing. That's why these regulations string us up tighter than any net. Fishing is not an everyday job. When the fish are there, you have to go get them. In December, when the mullet run ahead of a cold front, you can go two days straight. You never know what your hours are. It's not a set schedule. And the season is short. Blue fin tuna and mackerel favor water temperatures of sixty-eight to seventy-five degrees. Fisherman's got a narrow window, from Thanksgiving to Valentine's Day.

"Tying the Nets", 36"h x 24"w, oil on canvas

"Nets and Buoys", 24"h x 36"w, oil on canvas.

I read another report in a magazine. Written by some fella from the National Academy of Science. He said that eighty percent of commercial fish stocks in U. S. waters like mackeral, swordfish, tuna and pompano are disapearing. That may be true.

If it is, you can probably blame it on the Free Trade Agreement. Three hundred-foot freighters from Taiwan or some such place with hydraulic net openings, all sashaying back to a gigantic mother ship-factory that gets the fish ready for market. Forget radar and sonar. They got depth sounders, global positioning systems, computers, bottom fish-finding machines. It's not the little guy like me. Or even the recreational folks. It's these big guys, looting our waters. The fish don't stand a chance.

What's interesting is that fishermen started the whole thing, got the regulation ball rolling in the first place. It was 'way before my time. Seems like some outsider from up the East Coast came through the State, fishing our lakes with great big old salt-water nets. The locals petitioned their legislators to do something and they did. The legislature passed a law that regulated netting by outsiders. And that was the hole in the screen. If you don't want a houseful of mosquitoes, you keep the screen door patched. Better still, you don't open it in the first place.

Early sun hurts my eyes. That's why I like to fish at night. Going out to sea, one of a string of boats spread apart out of the mouth of the inlet, each fisherman headed for the part of the ocean where he hopes to find fish. So long as it's not the wrong spot, or the wrong fish, or the wrong time of year.

I like the night water best, swirls of phosphorus, one Milky Way above me, another in my wake. The moonlight glancing off the shell of a turtle, swimming back to sea from laying her eggs on the beach. Raccoons are going to eat most of the eggs. Only one out of a hundred will survive.

I'll bet you didn't know that a turtle's heart will beat for hours after it has been cut up and butchered. Me and my buddies, we're like the turtles. You may cut us up and turn us into soup, our hearts will still be beating. We'll still be here, dropping a hook over the side, making the line fast to a ringbolt in the stern.

"Fishy, fishy bite . . .
Your mother said you could
Your father said you would
Fishy, fishy bite."

FINIS

Philip Steel

Much of Philip's subject matter reflects his love of the sea and the people whose lives are affected by it. To paint the excitement, speed and grace of sailing craft as they move through the water represents a formidable challenge. Steel's ability to capture the power and excitement of wind and waves, ever changing play of light and tension in sails, rigging and crew is unique. His work is found in many public, private and corporate collections throughout North America, Europe and the Far east.

A resident of Ft. Pierce, FL, Phil took his Bachelor's degree in Architecture at Pennsylvania State University and his Masters at the University of California, Berkeley. In addition to a full schedule creating and teaching painting, he also continues to practice architecture. Phil is an adjunct professor at Indian River Community College and takes pleasure in conducting annual international water color workshops in such varied locales as Italy, France and Scotland as well as his annual workshop in South West Harbour, Maine.

Phil has participated in numerous one man and small group shows and is the recipient of a number of prestigious awards for his artwork, among them both First Place Oil and First Place Watercolor at the Annual Four County Juried Exhibition at the Backus Gallery, Ft. Pierce, FL, First Place; George Gray Medal Award for 2000 at the Salmagundi Gallery in New York, the Sanford Studio Award at the North East Water Color Society's annual National Exhibition, Kent, CT and the Silver Brush Award from the Florida Watercolor Society show at the Melvin Gallery, Lakeland, FL.

Phil is grateful for the continuing support of his wife and business partner, Joan Steel.

Evelyn Wilde Mayerson

Not content to merely live the life of academia, Evelyn Wilde Mayerson excells at living life to the fullest and writing about those aspects of it that interest and titilate her capatious curiosity. While on the faculty of the Temple University School of Medicine, Evelyn published two textbooks, but knew that her imagination could not be bridled by the confines of non-fiction. Close on the heels of her second textbook, she also had her debut novel, *Sanjo,* published by Lippincott. It was the first of seven novels, including the well-read regional compilation *Naked Came the Manatee,* in which she shared creative billing with other Miami-based authors such as Dave Barry and Elmore Leonard.

Evelyn is a distinguished Professor Emeritus of the University of Miami, having served twenty three years on that faculty, most recently as a Professor in the Department of English.

In addition to her novels, Evelyn has long had a love affair with the theatre. Her first full length drama, *A Long and Lovely Suicide,* was performed by the Reader's Theatre in New York in 1986 and was the winner of the Jane Chambers Playwriting Award. *Marjory,* a monodrama, based on the life of famed Everglades conservationist Marjory Stoneman Douglas, was commissioned by the Coconut Grove Playhouse and initially performed in 1996. Nominated for the Carbonell Award, the play was excerpted by PBS.

Evelyn is also the author of two childrens books, most recently *The Cat Who Escaped From Steerage,* winner of the William Allen White Award and published by Scribner's.

Evelyn and Don Mayerson presently reside in Vero Beach, FL.